The Little Old Lady
Who Was Not Afraid of Anything

by Linda Williams   *illustrated by* Megan Lloyd

HarperCollins*Publishers*

8   9   10

Library of Congress Cataloging-in-Publication Data
Williams, Linda (Linda D.)
   The little old lady who was not afraid of anything.

   Summary: A little old lady who is not afraid of
anything must deal with a pumpkin head, a tall black
hat, and other spooky objects that follow her through
the dark woods trying to scare her.
   [1. Fear—Fiction]   I. Lloyd, Megan, ill.   II. Title.
PZ7.W6668Li   1986   [E]   85-48250
ISBN 0-690-04584-0
ISBN 0-690-04586-7 (lib. bdg.)

To Charles
L.W.

To my parents,
with love and gratitude
M.L.

Once upon a time,

there was a little old lady who was not afraid of anything!

One windy afternoon the little old lady left her cottage and went for a walk in the forest to collect herbs and spices, nuts and seeds.

She walked so long and so far that it started to get dark.

There was only a sliver of moon shining through the night.

The little old lady started to walk home.

Suddenly she stopped!

Right in the middle of the path were two big shoes.

And the shoes went CLOMP, CLOMP.

"Get out of my way, you two big shoes! I'm not afraid of you," said the little old lady. On she walked down the path. But behind her she could hear

Two shoes go CLOMP, CLOMP.

A little farther on, the little old lady stumbled into
a pair of pants.

And the pants went WIGGLE, WIGGLE.

"Get out of my way, you pair of pants. I'm not afraid of you!"
said the little old lady and she walked on.
But behind her she could hear…

Two shoes go CLOMP, CLOMP,
And one pair of pants go WIGGLE, WIGGLE.

Farther still, the little old lady bumped into a shirt.

And the shirt went SHAKE, SHAKE.

"Get out of my way, you silly shirt! I'm not afraid of you,"
said the little old lady. And on she walked,
a little bit faster. But behind her she could hear…

Two shoes go CLOMP, CLOMP,
One pair of pants go WIGGLE, WIGGLE,
And one shirt go SHAKE, SHAKE.

A little ways on, the little old lady came upon
two white gloves and a tall black hat.

And the gloves went CLAP, CLAP,
And the hat went NOD, NOD.

"Get out of my way, you two white gloves
and you tall black hat!
I'm not afraid of you," she said,
and on she walked, just a little bit faster.
But behind her she could hear…

Two shoes go CLOMP, CLOMP,

One pair of pants go WIGGLE, WIGGLE,

One shirt go SHAKE, SHAKE,

Two gloves go CLAP, CLAP,

And one hat go NOD, NOD.

By now the little old lady was walking at quite a fast pace.
She was very near her cottage when she was startled by
a very huge, very orange, very scary pumpkin head.

And the head went...

BOO, BOO!

This time the little old lady did not stop to talk.
She did not stop at all. She *RAN*!
But behind her she could hear

Two shoes go CLOMP, CLOMP,
One pair of pants go WIGGLE, WIGGLE,
One shirt go SHAKE, SHAKE,
Two gloves go CLAP, CLAP,
One hat go NOD, NOD,
And one scary pumpkin head go BOO, BOO!

The little old lady did not look back. She ran as fast as
she could and didn't stop to catch her breath until she was
safe inside her cottage with the door locked.
She sat in her chair by the fire and she rocked and she rocked.

It was so quiet in her cottage before the KNOCK, KNOCK
on the door.
Should she answer it?
Well, *she* was not afraid of anything.
So she went to the door and opened it.

What do you think she saw?

Two shoes go CLOMP, CLOMP,

One pair of pants go WIGGLE, WIGGLE,

One shirt go SHAKE, SHAKE,

Two gloves go CLAP, CLAP,

One hat go NOD, NOD,

And one scary pumpkin head go BOO, BOO!

"I'm not afraid of you," said the little old lady bravely.

"What do you want anyway?"

"We've come to scare you!"

"You can't scare *me*," said the little old lady.

"Then what's to become of us?" The pumpkin head
suddenly looked unhappy.

"I have an idea," said the little old lady.
She whispered into the pumpkin's ear.
The pumpkin head nodded and its face seemed to brighten.

The little old lady said good night, closed the door,
and whistled on her way to bed.

The next morning she woke up early.

She went to her window and looked out into her garden.

And what do you think she saw?

Two shoes go CLOMP, CLOMP,

One pair of pants go WIGGLE, WIGGLE,

One shirt go SHAKE, SHAKE,

Two gloves go CLAP, CLAP,

One hat go NOD, NOD,

One scary pumpkin head go BOO, BOO…

And scare all the crows away!